Lavender 2: Lesbian Taboo

Copyright

Copyright © 2012 Spirited Sapphire Publishing

Cover and internal design © Spirited Sapphire Publishing

All rights reserved. No part of this book may be reproduced in any form or by any electronic or mechanical means including information storage and retrieval systems – except in the case of brief quotations in articles or reviews – without the permission in writing from its publisher, Spirited Sapphire Publishing.

Table of Contents

Chapter 1 – 'The Watcher' 5

Chapter 2 – 'Lap Dance' 12

Chapter 3 – 'Annual Check-Up' 22

Chapter 4 – 'Submissive Play' 29

Chapter 5 – 'Sister-in-Law' 39

Chapter 6 – 'Pagan Pleasures' 46

Chapter 7 – 'Camp Counselor Training 51

Chapter 8 – 'Glamour Shots' 58

Chapter 9 – 'Food Play' 65

Chapter 10 – 'Couple Swap' 72

Excerpt from 79

Lavender Love Diaries Vol 1: Lesbian Sex Fantasies 79

Available Books by 81

Spirited Sapphire Publishing 81

Chapter 1 – 'The Watcher'

Ah, there they are! The Watcher thought. Such a beautiful couple they were, her Maggie and Sue. It's been so wonderful since they moved into the apartment building across the way from hers. It's also wonderful that they rarely close the drapes over their floor-to-ceiling windows of their living room. She knows that they find the view of Chicago amazing, just as she does, but they have no idea that she finds the view of the two of them just as amazing!

The Watcher's parents couldn't have given her a better gift for Christmas. The high-powered telescope, intended to be for viewing the fabulous star constellations of the night skies, gave The Watcher an accidental….ok, not so accidental….view of some of her neighbors a few months back, and ever since she first laid eyes on the beautiful female couple across the way, she's been hooked. And, after the first time The Watcher bore witness to Maggie and Sue walking around naked and having sex, she has been a dedicated and very appreciative voyeur. Yeah, stars are wonderful to look at, but those sexy bare breasts and firm round asses of her obsessions were much more titillating then whatever the current zodiac star alignment happened to be.

It's Friday night, and The Watcher thought she saw Maggie and Sue leaving earlier and headed in the direction of what she knew was their favorite restaurant. She wondered if they'd be back soon to enjoy each others company at home, or if they were going to make it an all-nighter out on the town. Sometimes they did that. Oh wait! Is that them coming home now? Yes, yes it is them! The Watcher was suddenly quite excited, and aroused, as she realized it just might turn out to be a tantalizing evening of 'star body' gazing after all.

Ah, it looks like Maggie is putting on some music. Where did Sue go? Maybe she went to bathroom. There she is! She's coming back now. The Watcher notices that Sue is carrying a bottle of wine, or maybe champagne, and a couple of glasses. She is wearing a silky black robe, that is barely covering her perfect round ass cheeks, and as she bends over to fill the two glasses, The Watcher gets a grade-A view of that ass that sends some tingling sensations coursing through her belly. The girls take a sip of their wine and start to move in close to each other. Oh, it looks like they're going to undress each other. Sue pulled what looked to be a one-piece sundress over Maggie's head and....Wow!,The Watcher gasped in a whisper to herself. Maggie had on a really sexy, see-through black teddy that revealed her ample firm breasts! The Watcher had on so many occasions, fantasized about sucking, nibbling and fondling those gorgeous orbs. That body of Maggie's just didn't quit. Add with those long legs and high tight ass of hers, it was the perfect fantasy recipe that had given The Watcher many happy dreams.

Maggie untied the sash from Sue's robe and helped glide it over her shoulders, where it then fell onto the floor around her feet. Sue was wearing red tonight, in the form of a corset with a lace up front. Her body was rather petite in

7

comparison to Maggie's, but it was still breathtakingly gorgeous. Sue had pert little breasts where Maggie's were full and round, and Sue's legs were incredibly toned, probably because she took those ballet exercise classes. The Watcher guessed she did this for fitness rather than any real desire to be a professional dancer. Her shoulder length auburn hair was pulled back at the moment and The Watcher took notice of Sue's stunning almond-shaped green eyes. She could imagine that Maggie often got lost in those beautiful eyes, and it made The Watcher feel envious of the obvious harmony and connection of the two beauties across the way.

Maggie struck a wonderful contrast to Sue. Her hair was a wheat-blonde and cut in a short but stylish fashion. Her piercing blue eyes 'spoke' with depth and passion, as The Watcher had seen on many occasions when she was watching the two of them make love through her telescope. She watched them now as they toasted each other, and wrapped their arms around one another, face and lips only a breath apart. Their eyes appeared locked, and they seemed to be so totally into each other. The Watcher guessed that a slow song was playing now, because the women moved closer to the windows, and bodies pressed together, they began swaying slowly in an erotic hip grinding fashion. This was definitely worth all of the rushing The Watcher did to get home tonight.

Maggie and Sue looked so sexy dancing together like that, but it was nothing compared to the sparks that started flying when they began kissing each other. The kisses turned deep and passionate, as their bodies sank to the living room floor.

Oh yes, yes, The Watcher thought enthusiastically. They're going to have sex! This was just what she had hoped for. She readjusted her telescope lens so that she was getting the closest, most intimate possible view of the two women, as their bodies entwined with one another on the floor.

Maggie seemed to be taking the lead this time, as she moved her lips down Sue's neck and spent some time on each of her nipples, sucking them and gently pulling on them with her teeth. The Watcher absently moved her hand up to her own breasts, and started to lightly caress and tug on one her already hardening nipples through her thin blouse. She continued to watch as Maggie now moved her mouth from Sue's breasts down across her taut stomach, while at the same time unlacing Sue's corset, until she finally completed her journey across skin and lace, and Sue's naked body lay sprawled and glistening with moisture from Maggie's kissing and suckling. The area between The Watcher's thighs started to tighten and tingle, as if she could feel Maggie's mouth doing the same erotic dance across her own body.

Thinking in those terms, The Watcher moved her own hand down across her stomach, and then back up, as she started to unbuttoned her blouse. She managed to get it completely unbuttoned and removed while never taking her eye from the telescope and her unfettered view of Maggie and Sue. Now, she was able to unclasp her bra, free her aching tits and start playing with her nipples, while she watched the couple in her view finder as things really started to get hot and steamy between them.

Maggie was spreading Sue's thighs apart, as she slid the matching red thong down and off her legs. The Watcher felt a thrill of excitement pulse through her own body, as she watched Maggie skillfully use her tongue to begin licking and sucking on Sue's smooth pussy lips. As she continued to watch, she moved her hand down to where she could slide it up under her skirt. Reaching her destination, The Watcher wasn't surprised to find the crotch of her panties already slightly moistened from her growing arousal. She quickly removed her skirt and panties to have better access to her own pussy lips, and as she stood there naked looking through her telescope, she heard herself moan as her body was filled with mounting sexual arousal and tension.

Sue was moving her hips in a way that The Watcher could tell she was riding against Maggie's mouth. Ah, yes, she thought. She could almost feel Maggie's sweet mouth on her own pussy, as she spread her swollen lips with her fingers and gently began circling her hardened clit. Suddenly, there was a change in the scene. Sue seemed to be saying something to Maggie and tugging on her lightly. Then, The Watcher understood. Sue felt like she was missing out on the action a bit, so she was having Maggie change positions. Now, the women were in a perfect 69 position, and The Watcher could barely keep standing as she simultaneously watched the pair through the lens while stroking her now very wanton pussy.

Soon, it was easy to see that Maggie and Sue were using their mouths, tongues and fingers on each other. The Watcher could tell that there was lots of movement, and it seemed to be getting a bit more frantic. It only made sense that Sue was the first to reach her pivotal moment since Maggie had been stimulating her for a while. The Watcher saw Sue throw back her head, with her mouth formed in the shape of an 'O', and even though she couldn't actually hear her, it was more than obvious that she was in the throes of a very intense orgasm. The Watcher slipped a finger into her soaking pussy as she witnessed Sue's pleasure, and within just a couple minutes, her own orgasmic contractions began. Holding onto the telescope, The Watcher continued to view Sue thrashing as she, herself, clinched her thighs together, squeezing her hand as she rode wave after wave of pleasure.

Sue calmed finally, and went back to pleasing Maggie with her mouth and tongue. It was clear that Maggie was also getting close to falling over the edge of that cliff of ecstasy. The Watcher tried to keep her focus, but as soon as Maggie started to ride Sue's face, it was just too much for her. Rapidly finger fucking her dripping pussy, The Watcher lost all control as her knees grew too weak to hold her up and she collapsed to the floor in another, even more intense orgasm.

The Watcher tried to catch her breath quickly, but that just wasn't going to happen. It was several minutes before she had returned to reality, and was able to stand once again. She put her eye back to the telescope to get one more peek at her lovely ladies. The Watcher smiled slightly as she watched

11

Maggie and Sue, naked and arms around each other, turning off the lights as they strolled out of the living room together. Oh, how she so enjoyed these secret Friday night rendezvous!

Chapter 2 – 'Lap Dance'

Gwen looked at her face critically in the mirror after completing her makeup. I don't actually look 30, she thought. She had actually been carded the day before when she bought a bottle of wine. So she knew she was holding up well.

She knew this birthday had to come, but for some reason she was feeling old, even though 30 is so very far from being old and 'over-the-hill'. Was it because she had been single for far too long? Was it because she hadn't had sex in well over 6 months, and she was longing for the physical company of a beautiful woman? She wasn't sure, but, now that her birthday was here, Gwenn was pretty much ok with it. Besides, her friends were taking her out for what they called a "proper celebration." It sounded like it was going to be a fun evening, as it always is when they go out, even though they hadn't told her where exactly they were going. They did instruct her to dress "hot" though, and Gwenn complied. She now stood viewing herself in the full-length mirror of her bedroom wearing a sexy, white mini-skirt and a halter style top showing generous cleavage, and a toned bare back. Her sandals were Grecian style with lace ups winding around her calves almost up to her knees. The gold hooped earrings and bracelets helped complete her Greek goddess look for the evening, and with the contrast of her long, jet-black hair, she had to admit she looked pretty damn good for just turning 30.

13

Gwen checked her appearance once more, and with a nod of inner-approval, decided that she was ready for her fun birthday night out with the girls. She sat back on her plush living room couch and thumbed through a magazine while waiting for her friends to arrive. While waiting, she pondered just where they could possibly be taking her. She was hoping it was someplace fun and different, and perhaps even packed with sexy, available women.

When they girls arrived, they insisted that Gwenn wear a blindfold because they wanted the destination to be a complete surprise. So, after admonishing them to be careful of her makeup, she allowed them to blindfold her. They all had a great time in the car giggling and making jokes until Sharon, the driver, finally stopped and parked the car. Gwen was then led out of the car and across what seemed to be a paved parking lot. Suddenly, she was told to be careful because they were going down several steps. Her friends helped her navigate the steps, and Gwen's curiosity was definitely peaking, especially as she heard the growing noise of music. After what seemed like a forever-long few minutes, the group stopped and Gwen's blindfold was whisked off of her face.

"Surprise!" they all cried.

Gwen's mouth fell open when she saw where they were standing. They were at the entrance of The Grecian Garden!

"Oh my god!" screamed Gwen. This was exactly the sort of night she was hoping that her naughty girlfriends had planned for her. At 30, she really needed to cut loose and let her hair down. She wanted, and needed, to feel young and this was the perfect place to do it. What an amazing coincidence, that she chose to don her Greek goddess look for the evening, as she fit right in with all the other Grecian-dressed beauties.

The Grecian Garden was an underground strip club for lesbians, and was very popular among her friends. She had never been here before but always wanted to visit it. Now, she hugged each of her friends in turn and told them how thrilled she was with their choice of birthday celebration venue.

"Come on! Let's get in there and have some fun!" Gwen cried.

They all laughed and headed toward the entrance where there were male bouncers, the only males in sight. These guys stamped their hands and took their money, then motioned for them to enter. The place is jam packed with women of all shapes, sizes, ages, and appearances. Gwen loved the Greek goddess theme that it was all decorated in. She was particularly enjoying the waitresses. They were wearing short, white mini-skirts, strappy heels, and golden leaved wreaths in their hair. The best part, though, is that these gorgeous women were all topless! Her eyes were all over the

15

place because there was just so much activity and so much to see......yes, so very much beautiful, naked flesh to see.

Gwen was, again, thrilled to see that her enterprising friends had somehow managed to reserve a table just for them right next to the stage. This was going to be so fantastic! They were just in time for a new dancer to enter the stage and as they're settling into their seats and giving their drink orders, the music changed into something darker and deeper with lots of drum beats.

Gwen looked up to watch as one of the most beautiful women she'd ever seen strutted onto the stage. She was probably close to 6 feet tall, and wearing an amazing, and very sultry, warrior outfit. It was made out of a type of dark brown leather, low cut and very short. With gold details and a red cape, it was topped off with a set of matching wrist cuffs and gold Venus shoes. She was carrying a sword. Her long black hair swung behind her almost down to her waist, and as she moved about the stage and looked out into the crowd, her dark brown eyes took command of every woman she laid them on, including Gwenn.

Gwen was completely mesmerized, and instantly in lust with this woman. That was nothing, though, compared to the electrical sensations she felt surging throughout her body as the first pieces of the warrior goddess's costume were removed. The music was perfect for the way this dancer powerfully, yet seductively, moved her way across the stage. Her name was, appropriately enough, Aphrodite, and she was

every bit as perfect as one would expect. As she whipped off
the top part of her costume, she exposed a golden push up bra
that she used to show off her round, luscious breasts. The
skirt part was the next to go. Underneath she was wearing a
golden G-string that matched her bra.

Soon, Aphrodite was spinning around the dancing pole that
was placed in the center of the stage for just that purpose.
Coming off of the pole, she gyrated her sexy full hips and
perfectly rounded ass, while swiveling her sword in a very
suggestive manner. She made her way very close to Gwen
and leaned over just as she unsnapped the back of her gold
bra. Gwen ended up with two large, bouncy breasts inches
from her face, and, as if in a trance, she took a $5 bill and
placed it between this goddess's breasts, taking the
opportunity to brush the back of her hand across those
smooth, luscious orbs.

Encouraged by the $5 bill, Aphrodite stood up and danced
her way all over the stage once more with her long, toned and
muscular legs before making her way back to Gwen. She
spread her thighs just over Gwen's head and posed her near-
naked, glistening body above her. Sure enough, Gwen took
another $5 and tucked it into the side of the golden G-string.

Gwen's friends were watching the interaction between their
friend and Aphrodite. Sharon's eyes started gleaming with
the beginning of an idea. She whispered something to
Sabrina, who got up and left the table. In the meantime,
Aphrodite was coming to the end of her performance and

17

taking a final bow amid the whistles, applause and catcalls.
The expression on Gwen's face was priceless, and her friends
covertly sprung into action.

Sabrina had discreetly returned to the table and nodded
slightly at Sharon. Gwen missed it all, because she was still
looking towards the elevated dance floor and dreaming about
the very beautiful Aphrodite who had just adorned the stage
with her presence. Gwenn looked over at her friends and
said," Was she not the hottest creature that you've ever
seen?"

"Oh yes, she's a looker alright!"

"Totally gorgeous!"

"I wouldn't mind having some of that!"

There was a lot more murmuring over the incredible stripper.
Suddenly, Gwen looked up to see Aphrodite approaching
their table and her eyes lit right up!

"Good evening, ladies," Aphrodite said in a sultry voice.
"I'm looking for a birthday girl named Gwen."

While her friends all pointed to her, Gwen was struck
speechless. Oh, what had her crazy, wonderful friends done
to her now? Aphrodite made her way over to Gwen and took
her by the hand.

"Come on, Baby," she said. "You've got a birthday gift waiting in the VIP Lounge."

With that, she led Gwen away from her table of cheering friends, and went up a set of stairs at the back of the club. Aphrodite was wearing the cape from her outfit but Gwen could tell that she was still only wearing her gold G-string and Venus shoes. They walked into a main room in the VIP Lounge that held another, smaller stage, and it was like another complete club upstairs. There were fewer patrons up here, as well as all of these little rooms that cut off of the main VIP Lounge. It was to one of these smaller rooms that Aphrodite led Gwen.

There was a purple, velvet cushioned chair sitting almost in the middle of the room as well as a matching purple velvet loveseat and end table sitting against one wall. Aphrodite locked the door and led Gwen over to the chair. The room was seductively lit by flickering flame light bulbs on the wall, and sultry Moroccan-like music was playing through speakers hidden flush in the walls.

"Sit down, sweetheart," she said. "I'm going to give you a full 30 minutes of the best birthday present you've ever had."

Aphrodite started to dance up close and personal in front of her. Oh my god, thought Gwen, as her body immediately responded to the dancer's musky-like perfume and nakedness slithering just inches away from her. Gwen's pussy was already responding and moistening with her own sweet dew, as her hips rocked gently back and forth on the chair. This beautiful Amazon Goddess straddled Gwen as she performed snake like moves just inches from Gwen's body. Gwen's mouth went dry as she was biting her bottom lip to contain any moaning, while she watched Aphrodite's nipples come closer and closer to her mouth. Those luscious tits were within licking range, and it took every ounce of self-control for Gwen to keep from touching her sexy, private dancer.

Gwen wasn't completely clear on the rules of engagement in their private room, so she kept her hands and legs firmly planted and still. Ok, not so still, they were trembling with want. It got even worse when Aphrodite put a leg up on the chair and poised her crotch just inches from Gwen's face. She was so close, that Gwen could see the outline of her lips through the thin gold G-string, and she longed to explore them with her mouth and tongue. Still, Gwen stayed in place, trying to calm her breathing so she wouldn't hyperventilate from sexual tension and frustration.

Just when she thought she might die of pent-up pleasure, Gwen got another shock. While Aphrodite was dancing over her, she suddenly started to run her fingers over the outside of Gwen's halter top and teasing her nipples through it. Gwen gasped and arched her back against the chair, letting her body language signal the 'go ahead' to Aphrodite, however, Aphrodite didn't' stay there. She moved her hands even further down Gwen's body as she danced her way down to her knees.

She slid her hand up Gwen's mini-skirt and slipped a finger just inside of Gwen's thong panties. Instantly, she found Gwen's stiff little clit and started moving circles around it.

"Mmm," Aphrodite murmured. "You're so nice and wet. You must really like me, hmm? I bet you'd like nothing more than to feel my mouth on your pussy right now, am I right?"

Gwen managed to nod and groan at the same time. Immediately, Aphrodite slipped her head under Gwen's skirt and flicked the tip of her tongue across Gwen's warm swollen clit. Gwen gasped again and moved her hips so that she was riding Aphrodite's tongue. She still wasn't sure if she was allowed to touch Aphrodite or not, but she put her hands lightly on the back of her head. However, she quickly removed them because she was afraid she would lose control and push Aphrodite's head into her pussy.

Gwen was so far off in pussy wonderland, literally dazed and confused into a blissful state as she leaned back and received the most expert of tongue lashings. Just when she was sure it couldn't get any better, Aphrodite added another touch. She slid two fingers inside of Gwen's now very wet tunnel of love, and started to slide them in-and-out in time with the circles she was making with her tongue around her clit.

Gwen was starting to squirm uncontrollably, as Aphrodite rhythmically continued plunging her fingers deep inside of her. Oh my god, I'm going to cum, Gwen thought. I hope that's not against the rules! Just as quickly as that thought entered her mind, it left, as her body stiffened to the sudden onset of climax. She couldn't have stopped it if her life depended upon it. Instead, she grasped the sides of the chair, wrapped her legs around Aphrodite's shoulders, and rode her face and fingers for all she was worth.

As Gwen was catching her breath, Aphrodite gave her clit and pussy a final teasing lick and straightened up her skirt. Then she stood up and leaned down to give Gwen a kiss. Gwen could taste herself on Aphrodite's mouth. Aphrodite straightened up and smiled down at Gwen.

"Happy Birthday sweetheart. Now I better return you to your friends before they send out a search party." Aphrodite took Gwen's hand and helped her stand. With another quick kiss, she led the way in the same direction that they had come in, and back downstairs. She delivered Gwen, who was still in a daze, to her table near the stage and waved at the girls.

Gwen's friends started talking all at once, bombarding her with questions. She simply held up a hand to silence them.

"This has been an exceptionally happy birthday, and I've got to thank you for the greatest present ever. Now, order me a drink, and I'll tell you all about it." Then she smiled a private little smile because she knew she would remember this birthday for the rest of her life.

Chapter 3 – 'Annual Check-Up'

I wonder if other women actually look forward to their yearly gynecological checkup, Abby thought, as she made the 45 minute drive to Dr. Nichols' office. I really should have changed doctors when I moved last year, she thought. But I'm so comfortable with Dr. Nichols. She's perfect for me. She's a tremendous doctor; never mind that I'm unbelievably attracted to her. Again, she had to laugh at herself. Every time she heard women talking about how much they dreaded their gynecological exams, all she could think about, was how hard she had to try to not get sexually turned on during hers.

At 42, you would think that I should be past all of this "crush" stuff, Abby thought. It just wasn't that easy, though. Dr. Nichols bore a striking resemblance to the gorgeous actress, Maria Bello, only taller. Not only that, Dr. Nichols was British and that sexy accent drove Abby absolutely wild. Abby even played with the idea of getting check-ups every 6 months, just so she could feel Dr. Nichols gently hands against her skin.

Trying to tamp down her excitement, Abby checked in with the receptionist and took a seat next to an oversized aquarium. Why do doctor's offices have aquariums? Abby pondered. Was it to calm the patients? Instead of having a fish tank, why not have a mermaid tank, which would be much more hypnotic, she thought, while letting out a slight chuckle. Within just a few minutes, Abby was called back to an examination room. The nurse left her with one of those fashionable paper gowns, and told her the doctor would be in to see her shortly. She undressed and donned the paper barrier that is intended to afford the patient a bit of privacy and dignity. Sitting on the edge of the examination table, Abby mindlessly caressed the sides of her thighs while fantasizing of what it might be like if Dr. Nichols and she had some quality time together…...sans the paper gown. The very thought hardened Abby's nipples, and she could feel them chafing against the slightly rough paper material, which only served to arouse her more.

Suddenly, there was a quick knock on the door, and Dr. Nichols entered the room. She greeted Abby and sat down on the rolling stool next to the exam table. Her very presence was intoxicating to Abby, and she could immediately feel the heat of arousal flush her body. Dr. Nichols had an air of confidence and stature that was damn sexy. Then there were those breathtaking facial features of slightly plump lips, deep brown eyes and high check bones that made Abby just want to lean in and kiss the hell out of her. Abby tried to remain composed, as she rather absentmindedly answered Dr. Nichols questions asking if anything had changed since her last exam. Dr. Nichols then instructed Abby to lie back on the table, put her feet in the stirrups and situate her butt at the edge of the table. As Abby positioned herself, she watched

Dr. Nichols lithe form intently as she rose from the chair and stood by the table over Abby.

"Would you please open your gown Abby, so I can do a breast exam" Instructed Dr. Nichols. Abby was concerned that her now somewhat heavy breathing would be obvious, once Dr. Nichols hands began probing her breasts. Abby spread open her gown to bare her tits and still hard nipples, and tried to relax while secretly anticipating those gentle hands on her naked flesh.

As they continued to talk, Dr. Nichols performed a very thorough breast exam, which quite literally started the juices flowing in Abby's pleasure center by the time she had finished. Next, Dr. Nichols moved to the bottom of the exam table, and Abby took notice that Dr. Nichols had left her gown open, leaving her tits still bared. Not able to control her arousal, Abby flushed at the thought of Dr. Nichols about to discover her moistened pussy, when she continued on with the internal part of the exam. Nonchalantly, Dr. Nichols continued to chat with Abby as she put on a pair of latex gloves and slid a couple gloved fingers inside of Abby to check her ovaries and uterus. It may have been an exam to Dr. Nichols, but Abby could feel herself getting embarrassingly wet the more her gorgeous doctor probed her. She actually was afraid she might start groaning with pleasure if the exam went on much longer.

Finally, Dr. Nichols withdrew her fingers from Abby, and she started to sit up.

"No, no, Abby, can you please just stay there for a minute?" Dr. Nichols said as she got up from her little stool.

"Oh sure," Abby replied. "Is there something wrong?"

"No, no, Abby," Dr. Nichols said. "In fact, I think there just might be something truly right."

Abby watched as Dr. Nichols locked the door and then walked back over to her. Next, she took Abby's hand gently into hers and looked her directly in the eyes.

"Please call me Emma," she said, forming those lips into a seductive smile. "I noticed that you've become quite turned on during my examination of you, and I have to admit to a bit of an attraction to you as well. I can't possibly let you leave here until you've been fully and intimately examined."

With that, she started to unbutton her lab coat. The lab coat was quickly followed by the rest of her clothing, and in a matter of less than a minute, beautiful Dr. Nichols......Emma, was standing in front of Abby completely naked. Abby found herself caught between shock and uncontainable lust. Did she nod off and start dreaming, or was her doctor-patient fantasy actually coming true?

Emma's body was just as gorgeous as Abby had often imagined it might be. Full, teardrop-shaped breasts with dusky rose areolas, and suckable, puffy nipples that jutted out from a body with a curved in waist, slim hips and a toned, tight ass. All Abby could do was stare in wonder as this beautiful woman instructed her to keep her feet in the stirrups and lay back down.

Abby gasped as Emma bent over her and placed her lips against Abby's. This is something that Abby had only ever dreamed of, and the moment was so surreal, she wasn't even certain what was happening was reality. As soon as Emma slipped the tip of her tongue into Abby's mouth, she knew that this was definitely real. It was a moment in time that she would always remember. As Emma deepened their kiss, she ran her hands over Abby's exposed breasts and gently tweaked and tugged on her nipples. Abby could also feel Emma's own nipples, as they were brushing back and forth against her sides.

Only then did Emma break their kiss, and it was so that she could focus on gently sucking and nibbling Abby's nipples. Abby's response was to arch her back and put a hand behind Emma's head so that she could take her nipples into her mouth even further. Then, Emma broke contact with Abby's nipples and started to lick a trail down across her stomach.

Abby prayed that Emma's mouth might soon be on that part of her body that was so aching for her touch. As if Emma read her mind, she moved in that very direction. Reseating herself on the stool she had so recently vacated, she had clear access to Abby's neatly shaven, pretty pink lips. She didn't even need to part the folds that usually hid her clit. With her

27

feet still in the stirrups and her legs spread open, Abby's pussy lips were already parted, allowing Emma to put her mouth directly on Abby's erect little bud and start alternating between licking and sucking.

Abby was biting her bottom lip so that she wouldn't cry out in ecstasy. Emma certainly knew exactly where and how to touch her. Maybe she picked-up a few secret techniques during her residency. As she continued her attention on Abby's clit, Emma suddenly slid a finger into Abby's tight and soaking pussy. Being a gynecologist, it came as no surprise that Emma knew exactly where that delightful G-spot was located, and just how to manipulate it.

This became even clearer as Abby's pussy started contracting around Emma's finger. As her orgasm took control of her body, Abby's hips started to gyrate and she came completely off of the table several times. However, the thing that shocked her was that something happened to her that never had before. She actually squirted! To her total humiliation later, she realized that she had completely soaked Emma's face and chest. Emma laughed it off, though. In fact, she even thought that it was quite hot.

As the women cleaned up and got dressed, Emma slipped Abby a piece of paper with her personal cell number written on it.

"That's in case you don't want to wait a full year before seeing me again," she said as she winked at Abby. With that, Emma unlocked the door and went off to see her next patient.

Chapter 4 – 'Submissive Play'

Kelly was so happy to be done with her work day. Sure, it had been another win for her in the courtroom, but then, she never expected any less from herself. For that matter, neither did her clients. Kelly's much-sought-after services as a celebrity attorney did not come cheap. In fact, she charged some of the highest attorney fees in her state of California. People paid them without complaint, though; because they knew Kelly's reputation and that she got positive results for her clients. Yes, Kelly was a fireball in the courtroom. She was aggressive and very much like a mother lion where her clients were concerned. So, while she did charge high fees, she was worth every penny.

There was something missing in Kelly's life, though. More specifically her sex life, and she was taking notice to it more often these days, knowing it had to do with her always being "in charge" of everything in her life. And, while she knew she had to be in control in her professional world, in her personal world she wanted desperately to be submissive to someone and briefly surrender all of that 'I am She-Ra, hear me roar' business. No one knew that Kelly thought this way, though. She kept her fantasies about being dominated and told what to do to her self. That was the kind of information that could ruin her stellar career if it ever got out. Still, she really felt the need to unwind at the hands of a capable and demanding mistress.

Kelly passed by a newsstand on her way out of the courthouse on this particular Thursday afternoon, and spotted an alternative newspaper that she had often seen. It came out once a week, and contained all the latest entertainment news, food venues and alternative lifestyle happenings in the Los Angeles area. Suddenly drawn to what interesting tidbits she might extract from the artsy and culturally-diverse paper, she picked up a copy and carried it home with her. After pouring herself a tall gin and tonic and kicking her shoes off in the middle of the floor, she sat down on the sofa in her living room and started browsing through the paper. About halfway through, she spotted an ad for something called 'Madame's Den of Iniquity'. Now, that really got her attention, so she proceeded to read the entire ad.

It seemed that Madame's Den of Iniquity was in fact a high class lesbian dungeon, where women were invited to come and play out their fantasies of either domination or submission. Kelly felt her stomach tighten in excitement, as she read the general outline of 'dungeon play', and couldn't get to her phone fast enough. Making decisions on the fly is one of the things she did best, and calling to schedule herself for some 'dungeon play' was one of those in-the-moment, fly decisions. She called the number listed in the ad and made her reservation for the following evening, on Friday, for a play spot as a submissive slave. Kelly was given an address along with instructions to arrive at precisely 9PM. It would seem that her position of submissiveness was beginning already.

After 24 hours of intense anticipation, Kelly arrived at Madame's Den of Iniquity as directed, at exactly 9PM the following night. The address was located in an industrial park, and no one would have ever guessed this clandestine affair was housed here. It was easy enough to find, with an unassuming entrance to the establishment. Two other women arrived right behind Kelly, and the three of them walked in silence down a long, dark corridor lined with red lights, that opened up into a reception area.

The reception area was bare, except for a small table with a glowing lamp on it, and dozens of small mirrors that lined the walls, reflecting the red light from the lamp across the room like a dense red fog. Kelly was the first to step forward and check in with the Dungeon Madame, whom Kelly guessed to be about 50 years old, and still quite striking in appearance. She was assigned to a dungeon room and escorted there to wait for her mistress, being further instructed to remain standing in the middle of the room and not touch a thing. Kelly did as she was told, and as she stood there waiting in the dimly lit room, she took notice to the props, costumes and equipment that were lined along the walls. There was a collection of whips, masks, binding gear and gags spread across a long wooden table to her left. To her right, there was a smaller wooden table that was covered in various sized dildos and vibrators. And, in various locations on the walls, she noticed heavy-duty hooks that appeared to be designed for restraining purposes. I wonder which of these submissive supplies my mistress will be using with me tonight, Kelly thought.

Kelly's thoughts were interrupted by a door opening behind her, and a gorgeous, tall woman entered the room, stopping to stand just a few feet directly in front of her. This bewitching woman was a few inches taller than Kelly, had long dark hair, green eyes, and was dressed in a one-piece black patent leather jumpsuit, with matching black patent leather boots. The front of her jumpsuit was unzipped down to her mid-belly, teasing Kelly with a view of her half-exposed tits. Her mysterious mistress stood with her feet shoulder width apart, and looked Kelly up-and-down in a slow and deliberate assessment. This is what it must feel like to the many whom she has cross-examined in the courtroom, Kelly thought to herself. Now, the shoe was on the other foot, and it was Kelly's turn to be interrogated.

"So, you are Kelly?" the woman asked in a sexy, husky voice.

"Yes, I'm Kelly", Kelly replied in a surprisingly subdued voice.

"I'm Mistress Nikki, and for the time you're here, you have no name. You're simply my slave, and you'll do what I tell you to do. You'll speak when told and not unless you're instructed to. Everything I instruct you to do, you will do immediately, and without question, or there will be consequences. Is that clear?"

Kelly nodded a bit apprehensively, but admittedly, she was already turned on by this' take control', hauntingly beautiful woman.

"You will address me as Mistress and answer any questions with Yes, Mistress or No, Mistress. Is that clear?"

"Yes, Mistress," Kelly answered.

"Very good. Now, I want you to undress down to your underwear and then get on your knees."

Kelly didn't dare argue and undressed in record time. She was in nothing but her black push up bra and thong panties when she knelt on her bare knees on the cold, stone floor. She was vaguely aware of Mistress Nikki moving around in the dungeon play room, but she kept her eyes on the floor and waited for her first instructions.

Mistress Nikki approached Kelly and stood before her. As Kelly stared at the high heeled boots that were in front of her face, she wondering if she was about to get stepped on by them. She also heard what sounded like slapping or popping against the palm of Mistress Nikki's hand, but Kelly didn't look up to see what it was.

"Get to your feet, Slave," Mistress Nikki finally spoke. "Go over to the back wall and face it."

Kelly rose to her feet and went to the back wall as instructed. The same wall she spotted before, with all the hooks and straps attached to it. Oh god, Kelly thought, I'm about to be restrained. She was instructed to put her hands on the wall and to spread her legs apart, in a 'spread eagle' fashion. As Kelly assumed the position, suddenly feeling quite vulnerable, Mistress Nikki tightly fastened straps to both Kelly's wrists and ankles, securing her position against the cold brick wall. A hand came around her chest, and aggressively squeezed her right breast, while some type of object was being brush against her ass cheeks. What is that?, Kelly thought.

"Stick your ass out for me", Mistress Nikki demanded. Kelly obliged, and while still holding Kelly's breast in a vice grip, Mistress Nikki christened those ass cheeks with a snap of her cat-o-nine-tails, and Kelly felt the sting vibrate all the way down through her legs. Something told her that she shouldn't object, so she gritted her teeth together and bore that one along with several more.

"Now, Slave, that's a little introduction of what your punishment will be if you displease me. You're going to tell me "Thank you, Mistress! May I please have another?" after each lick. Do you understand?"

"Yes, Mistress," Kelly replied in a subdued voice. And, to her delightful surprise, even though her ass was stinging and hot from her slave spankings, Kelly's pussy was starting to throb….with excitement! She was starting to get very turned on, and was amazed that she was getting quite wet while enduring her Mistress's 'tool of discipline'. Being submissive was indeed, even hotter than she had ever imagined it could be.

"Now, I'm going to be untying you so that you can move to that long table over there. Go to that table and lay down on your back."

Kelly gave her wrists a quick rub upon her release, did as she was told, and lay down on the table. Kelly let out a silent gasp, because the table she thought was made out of wood was actually made of a dark colored steel. The coldness seared through her body when Kelly first climbed onto it, but her bare skin adjusted to it, the longer she lay there. She looked up and saw that Mistress Nikki had approached the table and was holding some material in her hands. She proceeded to use pink velvet drapery cord to tie Kelly's wrists to the table through special holes that Kelly hadn't noticed before. She repeated the process with Kelly's ankles. When Kelly was once again immobile, Mistress Nikki brought out a very dark black blindfold that she tied around Kelly's eyes.

"Now, Slave, you're going to be having a bit of a tactile lesson. I've always thought it to be so much more interesting when you can't see what's coming."

Kelly started to tense, but she was also very excited that she was completely helpless and not in control of herself or the situation. The next thing she felt was her bra and panties being cut away from her body, which left her totally naked and even more vulnerable. Oh god, she thought, What's about to happen?

Just as that thought hit her, she felt something hot and sticky hit her nipples. She bit her bottom lip to keep from crying out. The hot substance quickly cooled and left her nipples with a rather numb, pulsing feeling. After this happened a few more times, Kelly realized that her Mistress was dripping hot candle wax on her. This was really turning her on! The initial pain, followed by the tightening of the cooling wax, was intense and pleasurable, and made her nipples quite erect. Kelly loved the way it all felt. Hot wax connecting to her flesh from nowhere, and her having no clue when it was coming, or where it was going to be landing. By the time Mistress Nikki had completed the lesson in tactile experience, Kelly was amazed at how thoroughly wet her pussy was.

Suddenly, out of nowhere, Kelly felt the smooth head of what felt suspiciously like a dildo, teasing the pouty folds that hid her now throbbing clit. She was so aroused and wet at this point, that she welcomed whatever Mistress Nikki might have in store for her, and she hoped it would include a climactic ending. Kelly tried to relax as she felt the slow insertion of what was definitely a dildo, slide into her thoroughly moistened, already contracting tight pussy. Mistress Nikki dildo-fucked Kelly thoroughly as she squirmed about on the table. And, when she could tell that

Kelly was approaching her point of no return, she abruptly stopped.

Kelly involuntarily whimpered but caught herself just short of begging for more. Mistress Nikki spoke to her softy but firmly.

"Slave, if you want more of this, and you want to be allowed to reach an orgasm, you're going to have to convince me that you're worthy of it. You may speak."

Kelly let loose a torrent of begging, and said anything that she thought might work. She told her Mistress that she wasn't just a Mistress, that she was a Goddess and that she was privileged to be her slave. Then she told her that she wanted her Mistress to see how much she adored her and that reaching an orgasm would show her how much she meant to Kelly.

Kelly wasn't sure if Mistress Nikki bought any of it or not, but after an intense pause that seemed like eternity, she did go back to fucking Kelly with the dildo. And, this time she also used the fingers of her other hand to simultaneously play with her swollen clit. It didn't take long for Kelly to succumb, and her whole body arched off the table, pulling against the restraints, as she cried out and rode the pulsating sensations of her orgasm.

Mistress Nikki untied Kelly's blindfold and removed her restraints. She then instructed her to get up and get dressed. Kelly did as she was told, but she wasn't sure how she was supposed to take her leave. So, she took a guess and knelt once more before Mistress Nikki.

"Thank you, Mistress," she said. "I'm forever in your debt."

Mistress Nikki acknowledged Kelly with a nod, and opened the play room door, so that Kelly could take her leave. As Kelly made the drive home, she replayed the events of the evening over and over in her head. The verdict was clear.....submissive personal play was the perfect antidote to too much professional power play!

.

Chapter 5 –'Sister-in-Law'

Tammy gave her apartment one last look to be sure that it looked nice enough for the arrival of her brother Matt and his wife Rebecca. They had moved away from Colorado Springs, Colorado after they had married three years ago, but they visited Tammy often, and during these years Tammy and Rebecca had become very close. Every time they came out to visit; Tammy always insisted that they stay with her. She had a three bedroom apartment in Colorado Springs, and she used one for her own room and a second one for a home office. Her guest room was always kept in good order, and she made sure that it was warm and welcoming whenever Matt and Rebecca came to visit.

It was funny how Rebecca and Tammy had started getting along so well that they no longer needed Matt around them as a buffer to feel comfortable and have fun together. Most of the time, the three of them did a lot of outdoor activities together, like hiking and kayaking. They also had talked about going camping in the near future. Tammy thought that would be an awesome idea, because it would give her a chance to explore what was going on with Rebecca. During the past few months, she could swear that Rebecca had been flirting with her, and making innuendos whenever Matt wasn't around. It definitely had peaked Tammy's curiosity, and she wanted to find out more about what was going on inside Rebecca's mind.

Things like long stares at Tammy, along with Rebecca double and triple checking with Tammy to make sure that she liked what Rebecca was wearing if they went out. Then, there was the way that Rebecca was always complimenting Tammy on her outfits, as well as her body. She was always asking Tammy if she had been working out, and telling her how toned and shapely her body was. Yeah, something was definitely afoot here and Tammy was determined to find out what it was.

Matt and Rebecca arrived right on schedule. Tammy had lunch already prepared, so they all sat down in the kitchen to eat. As they chatted over salad and sandwiches about what was new and exciting, Tammy was silently recalling how Rebecca hugged her long and hard when they first arrived. And, when Rebecca hugged her, she had pressed her body against Tammy's not in a way that a family member would, but in a way that someone's lover would.

"You look amazing, Tam," Rebecca said. "Did you do something new to your hair? It looks fantastic! Doesn't she look fantastic, Matt?"

Tammy smiled at Rebecca.

"I got it streaked," Tammy replied. "I'm really glad you like it."

"Yeah, Sis," Matt chimed in. "It looks really cool."

As they sat there talking and eating, Tammy felt a sock clad foot gently rubbing her ankle. Ok, well, I know that's not Matt, thought Tammy. Sure enough, when she looked across the table at Rebecca, she was staring directly at Tammy with a slight little smile on her face. Oh my god! Tammy thought. Things could get really interesting here. Matt was oblivious to it all, or maybe he just didn't care. After all, he was aware of Tammy's sexual preferences, but he knew that she would never try to take his wife away from him.

Once lunch was finished, they all decided to load up their

backpacks and go for a five mile hike along one of their favorite wooded hiking trails. The fall day was gorgeous and warm, so it didn't matter that the hike took most of their afternoon. Throughout the entire walking journey, Rebecca kept close to Tammy, giving her lots of little touches on the arms and looking at her like she couldn't wait to tell her a secret. At the end of the hiking trail, they took a break in a grassy clearing at the edge of a small lake, where they laid out a large blanket so they could enjoy the snacks and water they brought with them. Matt finished eating before the women and decided to go for a swim.

"Why don't you girls come, too?" he asked.

"You know," said Tammy, "I think I'm just going to relax here for a little while, and enjoy the scenery. But you two go ahead."

"Um, I don't think I'm in the mood to swim right now, either," said Rebecca. "I'll just hang out here with Tammy."

With the girls deciding to stay behind, Matt took off to do some swimming and left the women together to chit chat about things that women like to talk about. They both watched him disappear over the hill, and soon they heard him splashing around in the water off in the distance. That's when Rebecca turned to Tammy.

"Tam, I've got a confession to make," she said.

"Oh really? Now this sounds intriguing. What's going on?" Tammy asked. Oh please do not tell me that you're cheating on my brother. She thought.

"Ok, here it goes," Rebecca said, as she took a deep breath, and let the words she'd been holding in, fly out of her mouth in one long-winded breath. "I've been fantasizing about you for months. And yes, I do mean fantasizing in a sexual sense. I don't get it, because you know how much I love your brother. But I can't stop thinking about you and wanting to be with you. Oh my god, I even think about you when Matt and I are having sex! I know that's horrible! But I really am so freaking attracted to you!"

Tammy didn't speak for several long seconds, but she coyly was taking in Rebecca's beautiful features, and thinking how lovely it would be to touch and taste her amazing body. Tammy didn't know if she was caught up in a moment of thinking, or not thinking, and then, she suddenly grinned at Rebecca and leaned over to kiss her gently on the mouth.

"So you want to give it a shot right now? We're all alone."

Rebecca now leaned in to return Tammy's kiss. The kiss got deeper and more passionate the longer it went on. Both women were starting to breathe more quickly and their hands were starting to roam. Tammy pulled her shirt off over her head, exposing her braless perky tits, so that Rebecca could experience putting her mouth on a woman's breasts for the very first time.

"Oh god," Rebecca whispered, as she hesitantly started to squeeze and fondle Tammy's tits with slightly shaky hands. "I've dreamed of touching you and kissing you like this for so long!" After Rebecca dared to explore Tammy's tits and nipples with her mouth and tongue, she looked up at her and said, "Your breasts are so beautiful and I love the way your nipples feel in my mouth."

She kept kissing and exploring Tammy's breasts while Tammy was starting to move her hands under Rebecca's t shirt. Being an expert at navigating a woman's body, Tammy knew just how to touch Rebecca to make her gasp and moan.

"Shhh," Tammy said. "Matt's just over the hill. We don't want him to catch us like this."

Rebecca attempted to silence her moans, but she was getting so turned on, she literally almost couldn't help herself. Tammy guided Rebecca's hand down to the crotch of her jeans and helped her to unzip them. Then she gently pushed her hand inside her loosened jeans and encouraged Rebecca to explore what was inside her panties. Rebecca didn't have to be told twice. She slid her hand down beneath Tammy's bikini panties, asTammy spread her thighs apart to offer easier access for Rebecca.

Tammy felt that it was important to show Rebecca how to please another woman, and encouraged her do some finger exploration on her own. And with that, Tammy released her hand from Rebecca's and left her to navigate her smooth pussy lips and pleasure center on her own. She might not get this chance again, and she should have the experience of feeling her fingers inside a woman's pussy that was not her own. There was something else that Rebecca needed to learn, too.

"Do you want to taste me?" Tammy asked softly.

"Oh god, I so want to put my mouth on you," Rebecca moaned. "Please."

Tammy scooted her jeans down over her hips and lay back so that Rebecca could get her face where they both wanted it to be. She moved the crotch of her panties to the side and offered her stiff little clit to Rebecca. Instructing her patiently, Tammy told Rebecca exactly how to lick and then gently suck her clit. Once she got the hang of that, Tammy told Rebecca to gently slide a finger inside of her pussy.

"Here, just slide it in right here," Tammy whispered. "Ah yeah, that's it."

Incredibly, Rebecca was doing such a good job, that after only a few minutes, Tammy was so hot and turned on, that she felt herself very close to cumming.

"Ok, Becca," Tammy said in a shaky voice. "I'm about to cum and I didn't want to scare you. Just keep doing what you're doing, ok? Yeah, just …like… that."

Tammy's orgasm hit her and she bit her hand to keep her voice down, so that her cries of pleasure wouldn't carry all the way to Matt. To Rebecca's credit, she held on and did exactly what Tammy had told her to do. When she was coming down off of that last wave, and her body relaxed, Tammy realized that Rebecca's face and hand were soaked. She also realized that Rebecca was trembling with her own need now.

Gently, she pushed Rebecca onto her back, swiftly unzipped her jeans and pulled them down, along with her panties, around her ankles. Then Tammy expertly started to tongue Rebecca's clit, and tongue-fuck her. She had to remind Rebecca once more to keep her voice down, and then she slid two fingers inside of her pussy while sucking on her clit at the same time. It took only minutes for Rebecca's body to stiffen and twitch to the unexpected orgasm that washed over her.

Just as Tammy was about to show Rebecca some more tricks, they heard some more splashing, and then Matt's voice calling out to them as he was on his way back to them.

"Oh hell!" Tammy swore. Then she and Rebecca both started rapidly readjusting their clothes while giggling.

"Is my face still wet?" whispered Rebecca.

"No, not really. It just looks like you've been sweating."

Then both women started giggling again. They were all sorted out, just as Matt reappeared into the grass clearing.. Looking at them a bit oddly, he walked toward them.

"So, what have you two been up to?" he asked with raised eyebrows.

"Nothing special," said Tammy. "Just the usual girl talk.", as she and Rebecca looked at each other and exchanged a knowing glance.

Chapter 6 – 'Pagan Pleasures'

Morgan was quite excited as she prepared for the night's Full Moon celebration with her pagan goddess spiritual coven. She loved that she and the other women switched around to different locations for these ceremonies and celebrations. It gave them a lot of variety in which to fully enjoy these celebrations. She was particularly excited for this evening, because they would be meeting at the home of Trinity, one of their members. Her home boasted a private well-manicured lawn as well as an Olympic size swimming pool. The entire backyard was enclosed with a high wooden privacy fence so there was no risk of being spied upon. But, the best part is that since it was a warm summer's night, they would be holding the celebration skyclad, which meant that all of the women would be participating in the nude and truly at one with Nature.

Morgan arrived at Trinity's house to find that she was the last one to get there. Lilith, Eve, Amethyst, Bronwyn, Lark, Raven, and Silver were already there. Trinity welcomed Morgan into her home, and then led her out to the backyard where the other women were already setting up flowers and candles for the circle. A small bonfire was started and the women enjoyed some drumming and music while waiting for the sun to set. When the sun finally did sink deep below the horizon, and darkness shrouded the night skies, a ceremonial circle was cast, and the full moon celebration began.

The moon was large and beautiful in the sky, and the ladies all gathered in a circle. At the same time, they dropped their long hooded cloaks to expose their gorgeous nude bodies to the firelight, moonlight and each other. They joined hands as they chanted and sang, while performing a special rhythmic dance, followed by a drawing down of the moon. As the women moved around the fire, the flickering shadows danced enticingly across their naked bodies, and all of the ladies partook in stealing glances at one another's lovely forms. Following this, they offered their special gifts to the Goddess, and closed the ceremony by giving thanks to Mother Earth.

After they broke the circle, the ladies all went onto the Florida room that was located at the back of Trinity's home, where they enjoyed the cakes and wine that Trinity had prepared and put out for them. As they drank the wine and nibbled on the food, the women started breaking off into small groups back out on the lawn, as well as around and in the pool. The night air was still quite warm, and the women were definitely in the mood to 'make merry'! These women knew each other very well, and there was always a lot of sexual tension and electricity flowing amongst them whenever they gathered. The fact that they were often nude for the ceremonies, only served to heightened the sexual energy that seemed to be ever present.

Raven, Lilith and Bronwyn were on a blanket out on the lawn as they drank wine, laughed and talked. Later, no one knew who started what, but suddenly, the women were joined in a three way kiss-fest of sorts. Lilith broke away from Raven and Bronwyn and started to work her way down a little bit, positioning herself directly between the women's bodies. Raven and Bronwyn were still kissing each other deeply, while Lilith moved back and forth between their luscious and beautiful breasts. Licking, nibbling and sucking on their nipples while using her hands to titillate and tease their outer pussy lips, heated things up even more, and it wasn't long before both Raven and Bronwyn decided they wanted to join Lilith in the fun she was having. Mutual kissing, touching, licking, and nibbling continued, with all three women thoroughly enjoying each others natural body delights. At some point, Raven was lying on her back and Lilith had kissed her way down between Raven's thighs, spreading them nice and wide so she could have full access to her pretty pink lips. Turning so that she was facing Raven's feet, Lilith was able to use her tongue to part those pouty little folds, as she then glided her tongue smoothly and slowly across every inch of Raven's clean-shaven pussy lips, which elicited much moaning and writhing.

Suddenly, Lilith emitted a little gasp and groan of her own, when she felt what turned out to be Bronwyn's tongue on her own wet little pussy. Looking back over her shoulder, she saw that Bronwyn was sitting on Raven's face while leaning forward to share her definite talents with Lilith. These ladies definitely knew how to have a good time with their special goddess daisy chain.

In the meantime, there was more goddess love going on, as Silver and Amethyst were enjoying some aqua pleasures in the shallow end of the pool. They were kissing each other deeply while their hands roamed over each other's naked body. And, in short order, their hands disappeared beneath the water as they started playing and fingering each other's pussy. Lark, who was sitting on the side of the pool watching them, was so completely aroused by this display of passionate affection, that she spread her thighs and began teasing her own swollen clit, and alternately finger-fucking her tight, soaked little pussy.

Somehow, Eve, Trinity and Morgan also ended up together on the lawn. As sort of a 'Thank You' to Trinity for hosting the Full Moon celebration, she was lying in between the other two women on her back, while Eve and Morgan were giving her stereo sex. Each woman was in charge of stimulating a side of Trinity, and they were doing it simultaneously. They started at the top of Trinity's body, and Eve and Morgan each kissed and suckled on one of Trinity's earlobes. Then, they moved their mouths and tongues to either side of her neck, and, the totally fun part started when they made their way down to her tits and were squeezing, sucking and tugging on Trinity's nipples at the same time. Of course, things got even hotter when they both finally ended up between Trinity's thighs. After first receiving some simultaneous lip love from both of them along the crease between her thigh and outer pussy lips, her clit then got dual action from both Eve's and Morgan's mouths and tongues. As they continued their combined combustible actions on her clit, they each slid a finger into Trinity's tight, moist pussy, and it was then that Trinity was 'thanked' with a full moon celebratory orgasm.

As all of this sexual action reached a crescendo, there were various cries of pleasure coming from the lawn and pool areas. Some of the women even sounded as if they were howling at the moon, when their moments of climactic pleasure hit. It didn't happen all simultaneously, of course, but all that sexual baying into the midnight air was probably arousing whatever wildlife may be nearby.

Now, this was a perfect full moon celebration! These beautiful goddesses had shown their love and respect for Mother Nature, and had ended the evening with the giving and sharing of the most natural gifts of all….the gift of their sexuality.

After all of the women had shared their pleasures with one another, they drank more wine, relaxed and just enjoyed each other's company around the dying bonfire.

Chapter 7 – 'Camp Counselor Training

Denise had a lot going on in her life right now, and it was for those reasons that she was looking forward to being a camp counselor for an annual summer sports camp for girls. It would be 8 full weeks of hiking, swimming, and volleyball among all sorts of other outdoor sports related activities. She used to attend each year herself when she was 12 to 17. Now that she had turned 18, she had been invited to become a counselor. She was thrilled to have something to take her mind off of what she had recently realized about herself.

Denise had always been quite popular in high school. Guys were always asking her out, and she would usually go if she liked them. In fact, she even dated one guy exclusively in her senior year, but she wasn't sad to leave him behind after graduation. She had finally given in to having sex with him because she felt that she should, but she just didn't feel the 'earth move', like she was told it would. In fact, she didn't feel anything at all. No arousal during foreplay, no desire to feel his manhood, and no titillating sensations during intercourse. In fact, it just plain did nothing for her.

Denise wondered if there was something wrong with her. While her female friends always talked about how much they loved having sex with their boyfriends, Denise tried to pretend and go along with them, so she wouldn't appear to be an outcast, but she just didn't feel it. In fact, Denise just didn't feel that type of attraction to the opposite sex period. It wasn't that she hated boys, she just wasn't interested in them in a romantic or a sexual sense. The truth was, there were a couple of her female friends that she would often daydream and fantasize about. There were also some women celebrities that she was excited by, and she had even started masturbating to their pictures that she came across in magazines.

Denise had finally accepted, to herself at least, that she was attracted to women. She was attracted to them in a way that she had never felt for any guy. After coming to this realization, Denise got scared. Oh my god, she thought, how will I ever tell my parents? She figured that was something that could be put off for now, and she would wrestle with that challenge later. In the meantime, there was something a bit more pressing on her mind. She wanted more than anything to act on her feelings with another woman, but she didn't have the slightest clue as to how to go about it.

Wendy was Denise's camp counselor trainer, and has been Denise's obsession for the first 4 weeks of the camp. She was 20 years old and gorgeous. Her body was fit, toned and tan. She also had small, firm breasts, that she never seemed to feel the need to restrain with a bra. It had been exquisite torture for Denise to watch this woman bounce around in her tight little tank tops, and short shorts while leading the girls in their activities. It was all she could do to focus on what Wendy was trying to teach her.

Things were particularly difficult for Denise when they went swimming or got caught in the rain. Wendy's perky dark nipples stood out like sharp little diamonds through her soaked shirt, and she was so comfortable with her body, she never seemed to feel the need to cover up. Wendy has also been quite friendly to Denise, which only intensified her crush on the older girl. Denise's favorite part of the day, was after they saw all the camp girls off to their bunk houses for the night, and the camp counselors and counselor trainees would then all go to the counselors' bunk house. She would secretly watch Wendy undress and get ready for bed, all the while quietly masturbating under her covers.

On this particular night, the girls had retired early because of an extra early wake-up call the next morning for an all-day rafting trip. They were all excited about the trip, but also really tired from their day, so most everyone was asleep in record time. Wendy entered the bunk house and started to undress for her shower. That's when Denise made an in the moment decision. She would follow Wendy and pretend that she was going to the toilets, which were just past the showers. In that way, she can get some clandestine looks at Wendy's nude and oh-so-perfectly fit body. Denise walked nonchalantly past the showers into the toilet, and when she re-emerged, she was stopped in her tracks by the sight of Wendy soaping up her naked body. Glancing over her shoulder, Wendy sees Denise starring at her. Then, Wendy drops a bombshell on Denise. She tells Denise that if she hasn't showered yet, she's more than welcome to join her.

Feeling herself both aroused and now slightly panicky, Denise wasn't sure what she should say….or do. Is she flirting with me, Denise wondered, or is she just being nice and offering to share the shower?

As if in a dream, Denise slowly nods and starts to undress. Before she realized what was happening, she was standing naked in the shower with Wendy, both of them under the warm spray of water cascading down. Denise was floating somewhere between terrified and thrilled, and was actually trembling a little.

"What's wrong, sweetie?" asked Wendy. "Are you cold? Here, get closer so you can have more warm water."

She pulled Denise closer to her and put her arms around her. Then she smiled at her and picked up the soap. Lathering up her hands, Wendy started to slowly wash Denise's shoulders and her arms. Denise's trembling only increased, but not because she was cold. She was feeling so many things at once, lust being at the top of the list. Wendy had no idea that Denise had never been with a woman before. She had seen Denise watching her and just assumed that she loved women. However, given Denise's trembling, she was starting to realize that this just might Denise's first lesbian experience, and she better go easy on her.

So, that's just what Wendy did. Everything she did was slow and easy. Just as she started to wash Denise's chest, Wendy leaned in and started to kiss her gently on the mouth, while at the same time she began soaping up Denise's firm, round breasts. The second that Wendy's mouth touched hers, Denise immediately connected with that feeling of 'this is so right'. This, she thought, is the way that it should feel during intimacy. Not bland and benign, but electric and explosive. She began returning Wendy's kiss with all the hungry passion that was in her, suddenly feeling courageous enough to explore Wendy's mouth with her tongue.

Denise felt as if her nipples were connected to the pleasure center between her legs, because every touch that Wendy gave her there seemed to generate pulsating sensations inside her pussy. She wasn't sure what a real orgasm felt like, but she thought she might be pretty close to having one. For the moment, though, she just wanted Wendy to keep touching her naked, wet body and kissing her. She also wanted to touch Wendy and moved her hands so that they covered those pert, firm little breasts that Denise had been craving for weeks. Wendy encouraged her to play and she was starting to become a bit braver.

The two women continued to kiss and caress each other, as the water rained down upon them. Denise felt herself starting to lose control, and her legs weaken, from the explicit and expert guidance her counselor was giving her. Wendy's hand then began to trail over Denise's stomach and straight down, until she found those soft smooth lips that hid her erect and very sensitive little clit. When Wendy's fingers made contact, Denise gasped out loud and groaned as she started to involuntarily move her clit back and forth against Wendy's fingers.

Oh god, thought Denise, I think I might be dying of pleasure! She became totally lost in kissing Wendy, as she felt Wendy's fingers working some amazing magic between her legs. Her breath started coming faster and faster, and her body, weak with pleasure, was being supported by Wendy's arms. Denise vaguely heard someone moaning, but was so overcome by all the physical sensations she was experiencing, that she didn't even realize that those moans were coming from her. Just as she started to feel that something was about to happen, Wendy slid a finger inside of her contracting hot pussy, while keeping her thumb pressed against her clit. And, then, it happened.......Denise was quickly pushed completely over the edge, and waves of pulsating contractions vibrated throughout her entire body. Wendy kept kissing her in an attempt to keep the sounds from carrying through the bunk house, as she gently guided both of their bodies down to the shower floor.

Finally, Denise came back down to earth and allowed herself to be cradled in Wendy's arms, enjoying those beautiful tits that were hovering just over her face.

"Oh god," Denise whispered. "Thank you! I feel validated, I feel exhilarated, and, I just had my first orgasm!"

"Well, sweetie, I'm honored I was the one who was able to provide you with your first female experience. If you're up for it, I've got some other things I can show you that I think you'll really like!" Wendy laughed softly.

"Oh, my gosh, do you mean there's more?" replied Denise. She knew that this was what she had been looking for, and no man would ever be able to give it to her. She would only find her pleasure in the arms of another woman. And that was more than ok with her!

Chapter 8 – 'Glamour Shots'

I really hope Tracy likes this, thought Claire, as she entered the photography studio. She had always wanted to do something a little wild like have a private glamour shoot done, but now she had the perfect excuse to do it. She had a new love interest and wanted to make a sexy photo album of herself to give to Tracy. This can't help but heat things up a bit, she thought, even though things were pretty hot between them already.

"Hi there, you must be Claire," said the pretty receptionist at the front desk. "Just sign in right here and come with me."

The receptionist stopped them in front of a door marked Private and opened it. Standing aside, the receptionist motioned for Claire to enter. Inside was a huge dressing room. As in, dressing rooms you see in the movies huge! There was a full-length makeup counter with lights, and wall to wall racks of sexy lingerie and suggestive outfits that promised to show a lot of curves and skin. Claire already felt like a Hollywood glamour girl just being in this room.

"Ok, Claire," the receptionist said. "You will be choosing three outfits to wear for your shoot, and you can choose from whatever is available here in the dressing room. You'll also have two personal assistants. This is Kate, who will be doing your makeup, and Rayna, who will be in charge of making

59

your hair look fabulous. So, relax, let the girls get you glammed up, and enjoy your shoot!"

With that, she turned and left the room, closing the door behind her, leaving Claire with her personal assistants Kate and Rayna. They women asked her if she had any idea what sort of look or persona she wanted to shoot today, so that they could assist her in choosing her outfits, and then fix her makeup and hair to match the outfits and intended look. It took close to an hour before Claire had chosen three outfits, and had her face done up as well as her hair.

Claire took a look at herself in the lighted makeup mirror, and couldn't believe what she saw. Her shoulder length dark brown hair was styled in large, slightly tousled waves that framed her face perfectly. Assessing her makeup, Claire had to admit that she had never seen her eyes 'pop' like that before. The shades of matte green eye shadow and black eyeliner, lined in a 60's 'cat-eye' look, gave such a depth to her dark brown eyes, that she almost couldn't believe it was her. Her lip color was a matted brown color, and because her skin had a natural olive overtone, instead of using a typical rose colored blush, Kate applied a more brownish-rose colored rouge, and the overall look made Claire look like a retro Italian beauty.

When Claire had put on her first ensemble and was ready to begin her photo shoot, the receptionist reappeared and escorted Claire to a studio set that was decorated like an upscale brothel. She couldn't believe how realistic everything was, right down to a sexy round bed covered with a red coverlet trimmed in black. Taking in account the sexy lingerie she was wearing, along with her new retro-glam look, Claire imagined herself to be a high-paid call girl, ready and waiting for her first client. The smooth sexy jazz music that was being piped in, certainly helped set the mood, and she couldn't wait to get started!

Suddenly, one of the most beautiful women Claire had ever seen entered the room. She had long dark blonde hair, bright blue eyes, and a body that instantly took Claire's breath away. She had to be at close to six feet tall and could have been a supermodel. Yet, she had a couple of expensive looking cameras hung casually around her neck, so Claire figured this must be her photographer.

"Hi, Claire, I'm Samantha, but please call me Sam," she said, extending her hand to Claire, who took it and they shook hands. "I've got to say you chose your costume wisely. You look quite incredible. I could almost eat you up myself!" She winked at Claire when she said that, and Claire had to remember that this was probably Sam's way of relaxing her clients and that she wasn't flirting with her. But it sure did feel like she had hit on her just a tiny bit.

"Thanks," replied Claire. "I was hoping it looked decent."

"Oh, I'd say it looks more than decent," Sam laughed. "Why don't you climb on the bed and let's get started?"

Claire got on the bed, and began striking the many poses that Sam was suggesting to her. While Sam was shooting pictures from every angle and distance from the bed, Claire was really getting into the moment, and embracing her inner sexual goddess. Sam was taking pictures in rapid fire succession as she crooned to her with things like "That's great, baby! Keep doing it just like that!" and "Come on, Beautiful, show me a little more thigh, there. That's it, Sexy, you're so freaking hot!"

Claire played right into her hands, and by the last frame, she was practically naked. She was down to wearing only a black velvet corset with garters and black fishnets stockings, and she was mostly topless, if you didn't count her arms crossed over her very ample breasts. Sam was easily able to make Claire feel quite comfortable during the shoot, and had talked her subject into some very provocative shots. Claire was tremendously turned on by Sam, and found herself fantasizing of what it might feel like to kiss her.

Sam approached the bed, and sat down at Claire's feet on the black shaggy rug that covered a part of the floor. She had some digital photo samples to show Claire, so Claire slid down to the floor beside her to take a look. As they went through the samples, Sam commented often on how hot Claire looked in the photos, and how incredibly sexy her body was. Claire kept giggling self-consciously, but she had to admit that Sam had done an amazing job of making her feel like a professional pinup model.

"Well, thank you for your compliments Sam. I have to admit, I've definitely channeled my inner diva today, and I can't remember the last time I felt this empowered and attractive." Claire laughed.

"Oh, you are definitely very powerful." Sam countered. "And, you're more than just attractive. You are downright alluring and hypnotic!"

The women's eyes met, as Sam leaned forward and pressed her mouth to Claire's as she put her hand on the back of her neck to pull her even closer. As they settled into a deep and passionate kiss, Sam slid her hand up the front of Claire's corset and began fondling and squeezing her plump soft breasts. Claire moaned a little and put her arms around Sam, pulling their bodies even closer, while caressing her back softly with her fingertips. Soon, those caresses turned into urgent groping, and Claire quickly helped free Sam of her shirt and bra, exposing her firm, small tits for Claire to enjoy.

The two women fell back onto one another on the black shaggy rug, and continued kissing and exploring each others bodies, with the fever of two lost lovers reunited. Sam then began removing the few remnants of Claire's outfit, teasing Claire's naked skin with her mouth and tongue in the process. Sam then stood up to shed her hip-hugging jeans and panties, then pulled Claire up with her.

"Here, baby," Sam whispered. "Go sit in the vanity chair for me."

Claire stood up, walked to the chair and sat down. She sat back against the chair while spreading her thighs apart, with Sam on her knees in front of her grinning wickedly.

"That's just what I had in mind," Sam said, as she buried her face into Claire's pussy. Holding her lips apart while flicking her tongue in and out of her pussy a few times, Sam then licked her way all around those pink pouty folds, where she then began to suckle gently on Claire's erect little clit. Claire glanced sideways at the stand alone mirror on the studio set, and got a bird's eye view of Sam's naked form between her legs, and her hand pushing Sam's head further into the embrace of her pussy. Just as Claire was starting to feel herself lose control, Sam stood up and straddled her. She balanced against Claire's thighs just far back enough so that she could continue playing with Claire's clit, while also inviting Claire to play with hers.

Claire obliged, and her fingers quickly parted Sam's smooth lips and found her clit, while Sam slide a finger deep inside Claire's moist pussy, and began finger-fucking her at the same time. As the women continued to please each other, Claire's now soaking pussy started to contract, and she began riding Sam's finger faster and harder. Realizing what was about to happen, Sam grabbed Claire's other hand with her free hand, and sped up her actions as well. Suddenly, Sam's legs squeezed against Claire's legs, and they both came within seconds of each other. As Claire's body convulsed in climactic ecstasy, Sam shushed her moans with her mouth and tongue, while pressing her backwards against the chair.

After both of their bodies started to relax, Claire and Sam lay back down on the rug, waiting for their breathing to slow and the world of reality to return.

"I'm not sure I can walk just yet," Claire laughed.

"Oh, that's ok," Sam giggled wickedly. "I,uh, have something to show you. I 'accidently' left my camera switched on video and, well, here's a copy of our special 'glamour shoot session.' This one is for you…no charge."

Chapter 9 – 'Food Play'

Renee was so proud of Tanya for finally going after her dream of being an executive chef. She had been telling Tanya for a long time that she should just go for it. This was just one example of how great their relationship was. Renee and Tanya supported each other fully, and were so emotionally and sexually connected, that their relationship had withstood things that had caused the breakup of the relationships of many of their friends. These two women had learned that you just needed to work together if you wanted a relationship to last. And they really wanted theirs to not only be permanent, but fulfilling in aspects.

One area where their relationship excelled was in the bedroom, although their sexual escapades didn't always take place exclusively in their bedroom. They both loved to role play, and most of their role playing consisted of a variety of bondage and domination scenarios, and they switched off taking turns being the dominant one. With Tanya's graduation from culinary school coming up, Renee had put together a surprise that promised to be a whole lot of fun for both of them, and it involved some role playing in a whole new way.

Tanya came home one night from school totally worn out. She just wanted to unwind, and was looking forward to spending some quality time with Renee. When she came in the door, Renee was standing there to greet her. Tanya's mouth dropped open as she took in Renee's outfit. She was wearing a blood red mini skirt, black bra, black apron and red heels. The colors looked great against Renee's shoulder-length, golden blonde hair and the look transformed her into one smoking hot kitchen goddess.

Before Tanya could form any words, Renee spoke first.

"Go take your shower, Tanya. Then, I want you to come back out here to the kitchen completely naked. You've got 15 minutes to get out here, and get your bare ass in the chair that's waiting for you at the kitchen table. Do you understand?"

"Um yes ma'am!" And with that Tanya scurried off to the bathroom. Even though she hadn't completely grasped what Renee was doing, she had a feeling that it was going to end up in some sexy playtime for the two of them. So, Tanya quickly stripped and showered, being mindful of her time limit. As she soaped up her body, she couldn't help but fantasize about what Renee might have in store for them, and the possibilities alone started to get Tanya's juices flowing. She dried off her body, combed her hair, gave herself a quick spritz of perfume, and made it back to the kitchen clean and naked, in a little over 10 minutes.

"Sit down," ordered Renee.

Tanya obeyed, and instantly found her hands being tied behind the back of the chair.

"Now, spread your legs apart." Renee commanded.

Tanya didn't hesitate to obey. As she spread her legs wide, Renee tightly bound each of Tanya's ankles to the bottom of the chair legs. Naked, spread eagle and bound, Tanya was excited, but also a little anxious of what was getting ready to happen to her. After Renee finished securing Tanya's body to the chair, she stood back to take in the sight of Tanya's beautiful naked body, bound and waiting for her to take her pleasure with it. Tanya's plump soft breasts were heaving slightly with either apprehensive or arousal, and Renee was looking forward to paying great attention to them shortly. Renee also took in the site of Tanya's well manicured mound, and delighted in seeing her pussy lips already slightly parted due to her legs being spread open and tied down. Oh, I'll be giving you lots of attention shortly little pussy, thought Renee, as she then walked over to the other side of the kitchen to retrieve something.

As Tanya watched her, Renee brought over a tray containing fresh vegetables, fruits, and food toppings. "Now, I may not have the culinary skills you do sweetheart, but, I do know how to work a little magic with food in a different way." Renee said, as she placed the food tray on the table next to them.

As Tanya was taking inventory of the ingredients on the tray, Renee picked up a jar of honey, took out a spoonful of the sweet, sticky treat and dripped some onto Tanya's mouth.

She then leaned down and slowly began lapping up the dripping honey from Tanya's lips, as Tanya let out some low moans of pleasure, as Renee's soft mouth kissed and suckled off the honey. Replacing the jar onto the tray, she next picked up some chocolate syrup, and drizzled it onto Tanya's plump breasts and diamond sharp nipples. Leaning down, Renee used her tongue to lick up every drop of the chocolate syrup then nibbled a bit on Tanya's erect nipples, while Tanya started to squirm in the chair.

"Mmm," Renee whispered in a husky voice. "So sweet you are. Let's see if this whipped cream will make you even sweeter."

Applying the dessert topping to Tanya's body from her mouth down across each of her breasts, Renee balanced herself by using Tanya's shoulders as a base, while leaning over her body and licking up every last bit of that whipped cream.

"Now that's what I'm talking about," Renee said in a very satisfied voice. "You make the most heavenly of desserts! But I've been a bad girl, and I've had my dessert before my dinner. I better not neglect my nutrition, so let's not forget our fruit and veggies."

As she talked, Renee picked up a sizeable carrot, cleaned and peeled to make it smooth, twirling it in between her fingers, as she knelt down on the floor in front of Tanya. With a wicked smile on her face, Renee turned the pointed end of the carrot toward Tanya's wide open little pussy. Touching the tip of the carrot to Tanya's pussy lips, she moved the vegetable around in slow, teasing circles around her hole a few times, before inserting the carrot slowly and fully into Tanya, who was looking down and could see the carrot as it disappeared into her most inner place.

Tanya was moaning and arching her body upwards, as Renee spent a few minutes slowly fucking her with that carrot, until Tanya's pussy was soaking wet. Renee suddenly removed the carrot from Tanya's pussy, and held it up to her mouth. After first sniffing it, Renee licked the moistened carrot up one side and down the other, enjoying the taste of Tanya's love juice left behind on it. Replacing the carrot on the tray, Renee then picked up a firm, unripe banana.

"I just wanted to get your warmed up baby," she said, winking at Tanya.

Spreading Tanya's pussy lips open further with the fingers of one hand, Renee used the other hand to gently glide in the banana, and as she did Tanya pulled against her restraints, trying to push her hips against Renee's hand. Renee pushed the banana in deeply, and then immediately pulled it almost all the way back out. She rhythmically continued to pleasure Tanya's pussy in-and-out with the 'food toy', as Tanya moaned and desperately tried gyrating her hips in the chair, as if trying to fuck the banana. Clearly, Tanya was totally turned on by Renee's 'food play', and Renee was getting quite aroused herself, as she watched Tanya's pussy lips grip around the fruit as it went in and out of her hole.

Renee withdrew the banana and Tanya actually whimpered in protest, causing Renee to laugh. She had saved her best surprise for last because she had an idea as to how it would be received.

"Close your eyes baby," Renee commanded Tanya, and of course, Tanya obeyed. Once Tanya's eyes were shut, Renee picked up a very frozen, and very cold Popsicle.

As soon as the tip of the Popsicle touched Tanya's pussy lips, she screamed and tilted the chair back, as she tried to pull her body away from this frozen assault. Renee managed to hold the Popsicle in place, gliding it inside even further, and started to lick up the dripping liquid as it immediately began thawing inside Tanya's hot pussy. Renee's tongue was moving back and forth very fast all around Tanya's pussy lips, and Tanya was trying desperately to maneuver her mound against Renee's mouth. As Tanya's clit now became the focus of attention from Rence's mouth, she could no longer manage to twist about against the hold her restraints, and instead, her body succumbed to the pulsing waves of contractions that first hit in the center of her belly, then deep within her pussy, followed by a whole body surge that caused her to limbs to stiffen and tremble. Her orgasm hit so suddenly, that even Renee hadn't felt it coming, yet she kept licking and suckling on Tanya's clit, while she managed to sneak the banana into her hand again. Continuing to work her tongue magic on Tanya's most sensitive areas, she also slid the banana in and out of Tanya's contracting pussy. After a few more minutes of intensive food-fucking, Tanya felt her excitement building once more. This excitement culminated in another rocket-launching orgasm for her, and when it did, Renee kept the banana moving steadily as she simultaneously stood up to plant a deep, passionate kiss on Tanya's mouth as she came, and came, and came.

Finally, Renee took the tray away and untied Tanya. Holding out her hands, she helped Tanya up out of the chair.

"Let's go jump in the shower baby, and rinse all of this food off," Renee said.

Tanya smiled at her in agreement, knowing that she would reward Renee's unique expertise with food play, with a sexy surprise or two in the shower.

Chapter 10 – 'Couple Swap'

Zoe and Brenda were quite excited as they were packing up their car for a weekend camping trip that they were taking with their friends Paige and Diane. The two couples met last year at the annual Womyn's Festival, and the four of them had really hit it off. They were thrilled to find out that they actually lived quite close to each other, and they've since spent lots of time together participating in all kinds of outings, including some weekend getaways.

As the two women packed the car with all the necessary gear, Brenda started telling Zoe about a movie that she had seen the earlier in the week. It was about wife swapping, and Brenda asked Zoe outright what she thought about the whole partner swapping thing.

"Now why would you ask me that?" Zoe smiled.

"Well, you know I love you, right?" Brenda replied.

"Yes, baby, I know you love me. And I love you, too."

"Ok, well that movie kind of made me start thinking about some things."

"What sort of things," asked Zoe.

"Well, 'things' like maybe being with Paige and Diane, and, uh, you know, like sharing each other. Do you know what I mean?" Brenda finally managed to get out, suddenly feeling anxious and worried about how Zoe would react.

"Oh yeah, I know exactly what you mean." Zoe replied. "And, I have to admit, that I've actually given it a passing thought once or twice before myself. So, if Paige and Diane are up for a little swapping play, I'm open to trying it."

"Seriously?" squealed Brenda.

"Absolutely. I think it would be pretty hot!"

They hugged each other, finished loading up their gear, and then got in the car to go pick up Paige and Diane. The two couples headed up to north country, where it was higher and cooler, and there were lots of beautiful wooded areas that were perfect for a secluded and romantic camping trip. When they found just the right place, everyone jumped out with their arms full of equipment, and got busy setting up camp. Once everything was set up, all four of them went for a refreshing swim in the nearby lake. As the sun started to set, they climbed out of the water and Zoe and Diane got to work building a fire, so they could get dinner cooking. They had brought along some nice juicy steaks to cook, along with some potatoes to bake and a salad in the cooler. Of course, they also brought several bottles of good red wine.

The women had all put on some comfortable clothing, and while Brenda and Paige set up the blanket, plates, salad and wine, Zoe and Diane cooked the food over the fire. Once everything finished cooking, they sat back on the large blanket and enjoyed all the delicious food and wine, along with some titillating dinner conversation. All of the women starting glancing at each other from time to time, with extended mysterious looks, and Brenda started to wonder if Zoe had already said something to Paige and Diane. She hoped not, but she couldn't be sure. Once dinner was completed and the dishes taken care of, the women spread a couple extra blankets out close to the fire, and they all enjoyed some more wine, as the night sky turned dark, and the air of unspoken mystery and anticipation deepened amongst them.

Zoe cozied up to Brenda on the blanket, and began kissing and nibbling on her neck, while her hands squeezed and fondling Brenda's tits through her thin, tight t-shirt. Brenda's eyes were closed as she enjoyed Zoe's nibbling, and she pressed her body against Zoe's, while her hands roamed over the curves of her hips. Zoe looked up to see both Diane and Paige staring at them with a lustful look in their eyes, and Zoe could feel the sexual heat practically leaping off their bodies. Thus far, no one had said anything, but now all four women were staring at one another intensely, and the sexual tension was so thick in the air, you could cut it with a knife.

Zoe cleared her throat and spoke. "OK, I cannot stand the tension anymore, and I have a pretty good idea that we might

75

all be thinking the same thing. Here's the deal. Brenda and I love each other very much, and we're also quite secure in our relationship. And, we've recently become interested in exploring some more 'open' sexual situations. Brenda and I are both really attracted to the two of you, and would like to ask you how would you feel about a little partner swapping tonight?"

Silence followed this little monologue, as if no one quite knew what to say next. However, all of the women began exchanging quick glances with each other, until finally, Diane broke the silence.

"Well, to be honest, Paige and I have actually taken part in a partner swapping encounter. We loved it and we would be very excited to do it again, if you're sure that you're up for it."

There were smiles and some giggling all around as the women 're-partnered', and Brenda moved onto the blanket with Paige, and Diane moved over to Zoe's. They had decided it would be better to keep everything out in the open on the blankets, instead of behind closed tent zippers. This way there would be no secrets amongst them, because they would all be able to see everything that was going on. Plus, adding the voyeurism factor, how hot it will be to watch their partners pleasing and being pleased by someone else.

Zoe and Brenda exchanged little smiles with one another, just before they each started kissing their 'new partners' for the first time. Brenda was completely lost in Paige the moment their lips touched. It had been a very long time since she had kissed anyone except Zoe, and she knew now that she had missed that feeling of newness that you get when kissing someone for the first time. She loved kissing Zoe, but there was something dangerously exciting about kissing someone new, especially when you know your partner is watching! Paige slid her tongue slowly into Brenda's mouth, and the tantalizing tongue tango that began between them, sent shivers of excitement throughout both of the bodies. The two women quickly undressed each other, and their naked bodies melded as one, as they lay on top of one another on the blanket.

On the other blanket, Zoe and Diane were also getting hot and heavy with each other. Those implied sexual sparks that were flying around during dinner were real, as Zoe found out quickly enough. Their kissing was deep and very passionate. These two didn't waste any time in getting their clothes off either, and soon they were lying naked in each other's arms, mouths connected and hands exploring tits and ass. Zoe and Diane were greedily trying to touch and taste each other's pussy, when Zoe happened to glance over at Brenda and Paige. Brenda was completely naked and lying on her back, thighs spread apart. Paige's head was buried between Brenda's thighs, and looked to be busily licking or sucking on Brenda's clit.

A jolt of unexpected excitement ran through Zoe's body, as she saw the love her life being pleased in such a way......and, by someone other than her! It also made Zoe want to be doing the very same thing to Diane's pretty pink pussy. She flipped Diane onto her back and started to feast from her body, beginning with her perky, firm little tits. She licked and sucked and nibbled on those hard little nipples, as she kneaded each breast with alternating firm and gently pressure. Kissing her way down the rest of Diane's body, she landed just where she had longed to be. Diane's musky aroma rose to meet her, as Zoe placed her face between her tight and toned upper thighs. Nothing turned Zoe on more than that special scent of a woman, as she skillfully pleased her with her tongue.

Brenda looked over to see what Zoe was up to, and saw her beautiful woman busily pleasing Diane's clit as she slid two fingers into Diane's pussy. Knowing how masterful Zoe is with her mouth and tongue, Brenda knew the degree of pleasure that Diane was experiencing, and it suddenly, made her want to taste Paige in a most urgent way. She maneuvered the two of them into a perfect 69 position, so that she could part Paige's pretty pink folds and start sucking her clit. She was excited to find that Paige had an oversized clit and sucking it was almost like sucking a tiny cock. As Brenda and Paige continued to give lip love to each others pussy, their bodies started gryating against each others mouths, from the mounting sexual energy that was surging through them both.

Their symphony of moans became louder and more urgent, as their voices echoed off of the lake and the surrounding mountains into the night. Paige started to rhythmically ride Brenda's mouth, as Brenda held on, refusing to let go of that tiny erect appendage. When Paige's orgasm hit, Brenda got a huge surprise. Her face was suddenly and completely soaked in liquid. It was startling, but it was also really sexy. Even while Paige was climaxing, she continued to lick and suckle on Brenda's clit, and a few minutes later, her own orgasm flooded her body with wave after wave of pulsating pleasure.

Zoe had glanced over once again to see what was going on with Brenda, just in time to witness her lover's orgasm. This caused Zoe to suddenly fall over her own cliff of pleasure, as her and Diane were both finger-fucking each others moist pussies. Diane could no longer hold back, as the excitement of hearing and witnessing everyone else's orgasm finally got to her, and she let out her own ecstatic cry, as she rode Zoe's fingers into orgasmic bliss.

The women all lay back and held each other, and after agreeing that a good time was had by all, the women rejoined their partners and headed into their tents. The excitement still hung heavy in the air, but this time it was between the original partners, who would now be enjoying each other privately this time.

Excerpt from Lavender Love Diaries Vol 1: Lesbian Sex Fantasies

Suddenly, Hannah sees a blue light flashing in her rearview mirror. Slammed back to reality, Hannah's mind is racing. "Is that the cops? Oh shit, shit, shit! What the hell was I doing? I don't think I was speeding. I'm wearing my seatbelt and I'm not drinking." Hannah signaled and pulled over to the side of the highway. She watched as the police car pulled over and right up behind her. Stories started running through her mind about women being pulled over on lonely night roads by police impersonators. Oh god! What if that's what is happening to me? She was fighting down her panic when she saw the officer get out of the car. She looked a little closer and saw that this police officer was a woman. A smoking hot, sexy as hell police woman!.................

...."Place your hands on the hood of the car," the officer instructed, in an almost soft and gentle voice. Now officially terrified, Hannah did as she was told. Moving her hands briskly up and down Hannah's body, the officer suddenly slapped a pair of handcuffs on her wrists.

"No! Wait!" Hannah yelled.

Coming up behind her, the officer whispered into her ear telling her that she didn't have to worry, that she was just getting a "warning." With that, Hannah suddenly found her body somewhat unceremoniously sprawled on the hood of the police car. The next thing Hannah knew was that her sundress was pulled quickly up and over her head, leaving her braless, chest bare and the only left covering her body was her lavender G-string.

Available Books by
Spirited Sapphire Publishing

Lavender Love Diaries Vol 1: Lesbian Sex Fantasies

Lavender Love Diaries Vol 2: Lesbian Taboo

82

Made in the USA
Lexington, KY
03 June 2013